The Piano Man

Debbi Chocolate

Illustrations by Eric Velasquez

Walker & Company
New York

Author's Note

I grew up in Chicago, the youngest of five children. My grandparents were musicians and dancers in the theater. By the time I was seven, when I wasn't reading, painting, or drawing, I was busy recreating my mother's childhood memories of the theater in my own stories. When I turned nine my mother bought me an eight-millimeter film projector. On Saturday afternoons in late autumn and early winter, when the weather was too cold for my friends and me to play outside, I'd set up folding chairs in my basement, pop popcorn, and sell tickets to my "movie theater" to all the kids in the neighborhood. Later, I turned to music and became an accomplished musician.

I've always wanted to sit down and recreate the theater in the stories that my mother passed along to me as a child. I hope you enjoy reading this story about my grandfather Sherman L. Robinson, the piano man, as much as I enjoyed writing it.

Text copyright © 1998 by Debbi Chocolate
Illustrations copyright © 1998 by Eric Velasquez

First published in the United States of America in 1998
by Walker Publishing Company, Inc.; first paperback edition published in 2000.
Published simultaneously in Canada by
Fitzhenry and Whiteside, Markham, Ontario L3R 4T8

Library of Congress Cataloging-in-Publication Data
Chocolate, Deborah M. Newton.
The piano man/Debbi Chocolate; illustrations by Eric Velasquez.
p. cm.
Summary: A young Afro-American girl recalls the life story of her
grandfather who performed in vaudeville and played piano for the silent movies.
ISBN 0-8027-8646-4 (hardcover). –ISBN 0-8027-8647-2 (reinforced)
[1. Grandfathers—Fiction. 2. Pianists—Fiction. 3. Silent films—Fiction.
4. Afro-Americans—Fiction.] I.Velasquez, Eric, ill. II. Title.
PZ7.C44624Pi 1998
[E]—DC21   97-22668
CIP
AC

ISBN 0-8027-7578-0 (paperback)

Book design by Marva J. Martin

Printed in Hong Kong
2 4 6 8 10 9 7 5 3

For Mama,
and for my grandfather,
Sherman L. Robinson,
the piano man.
–D. C.

For my parents,
Chu and Carmen Lydia,
and my wife, Debbie.
– E. V.

My grandfather played piano for the silent movies. He wore a bowler hat, a starched collar, and fancy shirt garters on his sleeves.

When there was a pie-throwing scene, my grandfather tickled as silly a tune as you'd ever hear. He made audiences bowl over with laughter.

When the hero got one last kiss, the whole theater sighed as my grandfather played sweetly, tenderly.

When there were monsters on the screen, my grandfather played thrilling themes from *Phantom of the Opera*. People said my grandfather's playing made their hair rise and sent chills up their spines.

Years later, my grandfather played piano on Broadway with the Follies. He was called "professor" because he knew more about music than even Mr. Ziegfeld.

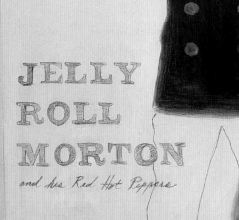

LAFAYETTE
THEATRE
7TH AVE. AT 131st ST.   LIBERTIES OF COLOUR 1968

One Week Only Com. Mon. Jan. 1

JELLY

ROLL

MORTON

and his Red Hot Peppers

My grandfather loved ragtime music, and he learned to play its crazy rhythms from the masters.

Jelly Roll Morton taught my grandfather to play two pianos at the same time. One with each hand.

And the "King of Rag," Scott Joplin, showed him how to play a lightning-fast "Maple Leaf Rag."

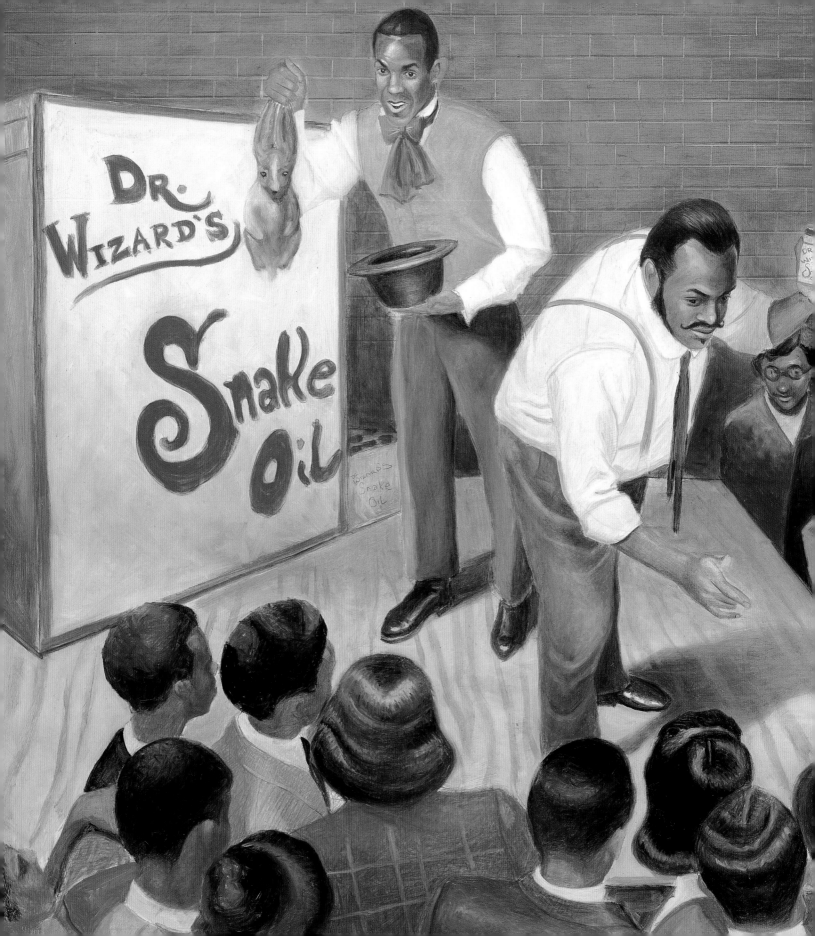

My grandfather played Joplin's rags on the road when he traveled with the Snake Doctor's medicine show.

In between songs he performed daring feats, pitched snake oil, and pulled rabbits out of hats.

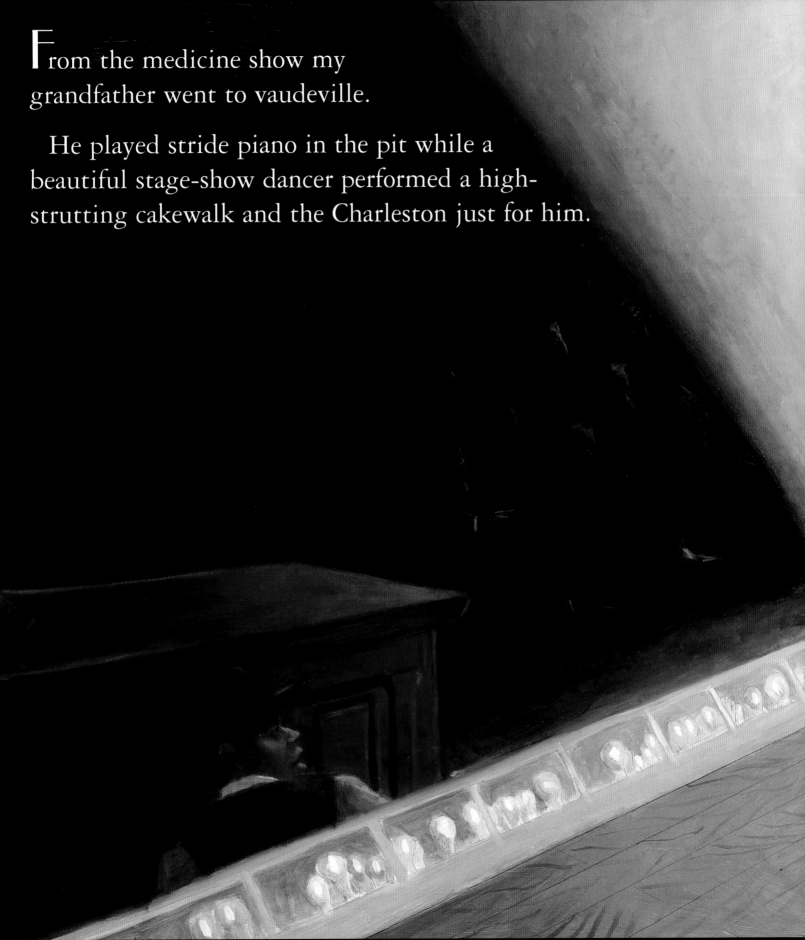

From the medicine show my grandfather went to vaudeville.

He played stride piano in the pit while a beautiful stage-show dancer performed a high-strutting cakewalk and the Charleston just for him.

When the piano man and the dancer fell in love, they were married by the Snake Doctor—who was also a Justice of the Peace.

After their wedding, my grandfather and grandmother performed musical comedies in ballrooms and theaters from the Carolinas to Arkansas.

After years of playing vaudeville, my grandfather and grandmother had a baby girl. Now they needed a place to call home. So my grandfather went back to playing piano for the silent movies.

When my mother was still a little girl, she'd sit next to my grandfather at Saturday matinees while he'd play romping chords to the thriller-diller chase scenes flashing across the big silver screen.

Then one day a new movie came out. A movie with sound.
People flocked to the theaters to hear the new pictures talk.
One by one piano players lost their theater jobs.
One day the manager of the Rialto
told my grandfather
he didn't need
him anymore.

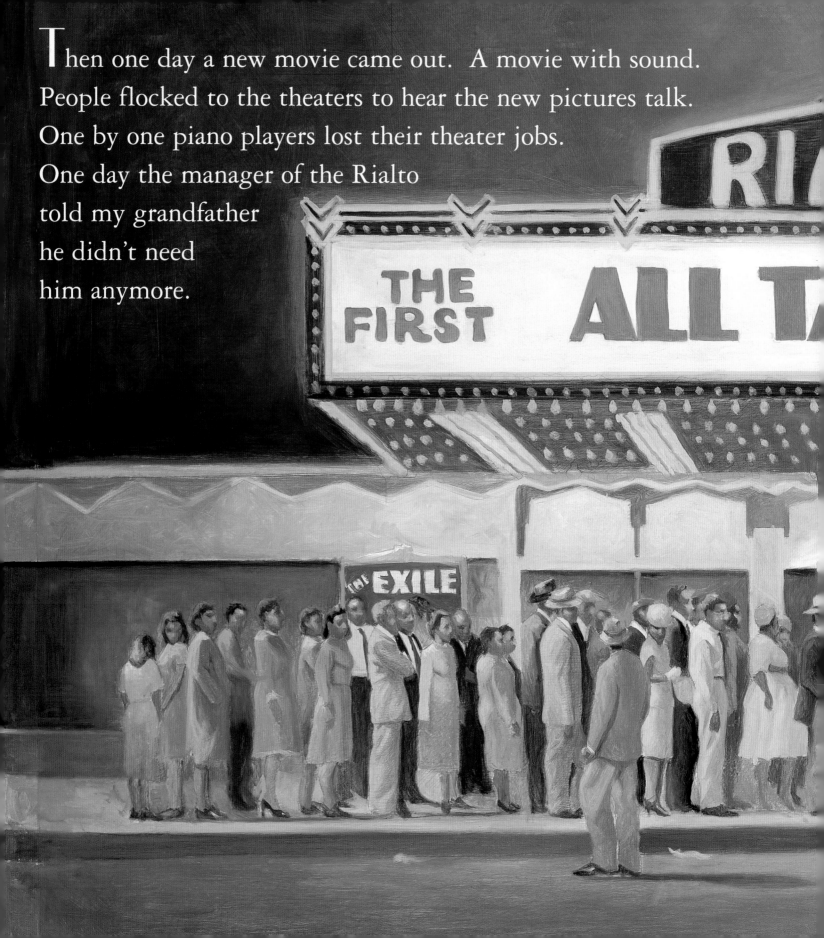

With tears in his eyes, my grandfather played the theater's piano one last time. Then he packed up his sheet music, buried his hands inside his pockets, and went home.

After the talkies came out, my grandfather worked as a piano tuner. Whenever his fingers stroked the ivory keys, my grandfather thumped out foot-stomping rags from his days in vaudeville and the silent movies.

My grandfather had silver hair by the time I was born, and he didn't tune pianos anymore. But he did tell me all there was to know about silent movies, medicine shows, vaudeville, and ragtime music.

My grandfather wasn't the only one who remembered those Saturday afternoons at the movies. Charlie Chaplin, Will Rogers, and Bill Pickett were forever a part of my mother's childhood memories. Then one day my mother saw a "for sale" sign on the old Rialto Theater.

Ever since she had been a little girl, my mother had saved money for something very, very special. For his seventy-fifth birthday, my mother bought my grandfather the old upright piano that had been tucked away in the theater's basement for years.

From that day on, whenever my grandfather was feeling sad, he'd turn on the television to an old cowboy movie. With me on the bench beside him and the television volume turned down low, the piano man would sit at his piano and hammer out his memories of the old silent picture shows.